A Compilation of Short Stories

by Michael Peron

ISBN-13: 978-0-9863143-2-2

Dedicated to all my patrons.
Thank you for supporting me!

Conception

He inspected the face in front of him with careful precision. The hair was dark brown and thick, flowing in loose curls just past the shoulders. The nose, protruding slightly to the left, gave a hint of asymmetry. And of course the eyes. Their green hue was familiar, reassuring. The eyes were his favorite.

"Jeremy?"

His wife's face changed, the features rearranging to display her concern.

"Are you okay?"

She edged a little closer on her pillow, and he felt the heat of her body underneath the covers.

"I just like looking at you," he answered.

He watched her lips form a smile and couldn't help but reciprocate.

That's my wife, he thought. She is so beautiful.

***

He stood in his office, waiting for the results. A screen was propped up on his chest-high desk, the only piece of furniture in the room. Jeremy preferred to stand, it was healthier. Especially with the amount of time he was working.

A tone went off as the screen changed to the results. Jeremy sighed. The test had failed.

He scrolled up to look over the data once more. So many variables, so many possibilities. At times he wondered if it was even possible.

He closed his eyes for a moment, trying to clear his mind. He shouldn't be too hard on himself. This was a monumental task. Most importantly, he was getting closer. He could feel it.

***

The robot entered the office and stood just inside the doorway.

"How may I be of service, Jeremy?"

"I have a few modifications I want you to make."

"Of course, Jeremy."

The robot extended an arm and connected to Jeremy's workspace. After a few seconds, the instructions were downloaded and the robot disconnected.

"When would you like me to make these modifications, Jeremy?"

"Now, please."

"Of course, Jeremy."

The robot walked out of the office and Jeremy's work for the day was finished. All that was left was to wait for the modifications to be made.

This was his least favorite part of the day. He hated waiting.

***

"How was work today?"

Her voice made Jeremy pause, the razor halfway up his cheek as he turned to look at her. She was back later than he had expected.

"Good. We're getting closer."

He finished the last swipe and ran the blade under the sink.

Her hand caressed his freshly shaven cheek, gently guiding his face to hers. He dropped the razor in the basin and met her lips.

Then he felt it: a hint of doubt, a hint of shame. Always the first kiss after work.

She pulled back for a second, her eyes searching his. Did she sense his hesitation?

If she did, she didn't say anything. She pulled him in closer, her hands exploring his body. The doubt melted away and Jeremy felt his heart racing, felt the desire growing within him.

They stumbled into the bedroom with the sink still running.

***

Cereal for breakfast, his favorite kind. Jeremy held a spoonful above the bowl and stared at it. He had had it every day for years and had never gotten sick of it. He was a creature of habit.

He put the spoon in his mouth and chewed the crunchy pieces before swallowing. The taste was familiar, reassuring.

"How's the cereal?"

She came and sat across from him, smiling. He looked at her face, following the contours of the nose, the cheeks, the eyes.

That's my wife, he thought. She is so beautiful.

"Good as always."

He didn't want to go to work.

***

He poured over yesterday's data, searching for clues, searching for answers. Every day he ran a new test, and every day he failed. At first the problems were easy to spot, their solutions simple. But those days were long gone.

It didn't help that he was working out of his home with nothing more than a robot to help. He wished he had a team, wished he had a lab. It was hard enough trying to solve this incredibly complex problem on its own, but he was doing it with his hands tied behind his back.

But Jeremy was the leading expert in his field. He knew he could figure it out, he just had to keep at it.

***

"How was work today?"

She smiled over the dinner table, but she already knew the answer.

"No luck."

He saw the concern again, the rearranging facial expression.

"But you're getting closer?"

He gave her a reassuring smile.

"We're getting closer."

He knew what came next. She would get up just as he finished dinner, the last bite entering his mouth as she stood. She would take a few steps, along the length of the dinner table, until she was standing next to him. For a moment, they would look at one another, and he would stare into those green eyes. The eyes were his favorite.

Then she would lean over and give him a kiss.

And with it, a hint of doubt, a hint of shame. Always the first kiss after work.

***

He lay in bed with his eyes wide open, his mind racing through memories, memories he didn't necessarily want to relive.

A long time ago, he didn't work alone. A long time ago, he had colleagues, he had a lab. He was an established scientist, with an outstanding résumé. Back then, he was never afraid to break new ground.

Until one day, he was told he had gone too far. One day, he lost his job and his reputation.

He turned onto his side, facing his wife. The sheets were still damp from their sweat.

Good riddance, Jeremy thought. He spent every night with a beautiful woman and he was worried about having a lab?

***

He stood in his office, waiting for the results. The window along the wall looked out into his yard, an assortment of plants maintained in near-perfection. He looked at the neatly trimmed hedges, the precise arrangement of flowers.

A tone went off and brought his attention back to the screen. Jeremy sighed. The test had failed.

He hated to admit it but he was running out of ideas. There were only so many things he could change about the design, so many things within his control.

Control. He looked back out the window. The garden view calmed him, its order and predictability in tune with his own penchant for patterns. It was a view he had seen for many years, as consistent as his cereal.

It wasn't the design that needed changing.

He pulled up a separate data set, one he hadn't edited in a long time.

***

The robot entered the office and stood just inside the doorway.

"How may I be of service, Jeremy?"

He stared at the robot for a moment.

"You know what I want."

He was invigorated by his idea, his new approach to the problem. Habits be damned.

"Of course, Jeremy."

The robot extended an arm and downloaded its instructions.

"When would you like me to make these modifications, Jeremy?"

He let out an amused chuckle. The robot waited patiently for its orders.

"Now, please."

"Of course, Jeremy."

Change was good, even for a man of habit. Especially for a man of habit.

***

Jeremy felt the heat of her body against his, the layer of sweat between them. That evening, his wife hadn't asked him how it went today. She had skipped over the pleasantries and pulled him upstairs.

They tumbled over and she squeezed her thighs around him. The pressure of her legs was intoxicating. She leaned forward and pressed down with her hips, pushing him in deeper. He saw a desire in her eyes that fueled his lust like nothing before. He struggled to hold on to the moment but it was of no use. An eruption of euphoria washed over him, stronger than anything he had ever felt.

Change was good.

***

That night, he didn't sleep. He tossed and turned, then left the bedroom to go to his office. But the results wouldn't be in for many hours. There was nothing he could do but wait.

He hated waiting.

Outside was darkness, but he could hear the robot doing its work in the garden. When the sun finally started its ascent, he saw a brand new arrangement, a totally different pattern.

A tone went off as the screen changed to the results. The test had succeeded.

Years of work had led up to this moment, so many struggles, so many problems. Finally, an android womb had been impregnated by human sperm.

He looked out at the garden and smiled.

He was a father.

Footsteps

I stepped into the dull gray cylinder, avoiding the eyes of the woman inside. You never knew if someone was going to try to chat you up, tell you about their day. I didn't want to hear it—to pretend that I cared.

I turned to face the opening and watched the doors shut, the outside world replaced by a blurred, aluminum reflection. There was a panel of buttons to the right, small circles numbered 0 to 22. One was lit: the number 15, first button of the sixth row. That number told me everything I needed to know about that woman's day, she had no need to tell me herself.

There was a distant sound of machinery accompanied by a slight jostle, then we began our descent. A smile crossed my face. This was my favorite feeling, my favorite part of the day. Going down meant one thing: I was going home.

We slowed down as the screen above the door read 13, and I felt a trace of anger at the interruption. The elevator came to a stop at 15, the doors opening with a faint ding. The woman walked out, turning toward me as she left. I averted my eyes.

While the doors closed, I pressed the last button—the one whose number was least faded, the middle button of the eight row: 22. It lit up at my touch, another faint ding sounding off in the metal cylinder. Then I heard the machinery, felt the jostle, and my downward journey continued.

Many years ago, these elevators were full of people heading down to the mines. But I didn't remember those days—I was barely two when the mines were shut. The Ardo Station I knew was empty, falling apart. Glory was long gone from its halls.

The screen read 20 and I felt deceleration once more, this time without anger. I was done up top, done with other people. The elevator came to a stop at 22 and the aluminum opened before me, revealing the lowest level of Ardo Station. Home sweet home.

A layer of fog poured through the door, the warm vapor tickling my legs, beckoning me to enter the dimly lit corridor. When the mines were in use, steam would help maintain the temperature of the halls. Thirty-something years later, that steam continued to cycle through the 22nd floor, a warm mist spread throughout my home.

I stepped into the corridor, a light flickering off to my right. No doubt it would go out soon, and no doubt it would stay that way. No one cared to fix anything down here. After all, no one cared to come down here. No one except me.

The corridor split in three directions and I went right, under the dying bulb. The 22nd floor was a maze of such dimly lit corridors, most of them ending with a thick steel door. Those doors used to lead to the mines themselves, the excavated portions of Ardo. Now they were welded shut, long forgotten under the twenty-one other floors.

I took the next right, then an immediate left. With most of the lights dimmed or broken and vapor thickening the air, I could barely see two meters ahead of me. But I knew where each of the corridors led, knew their layout by heart. This was where I spent most of my time: tucked away in a dark, forgotten corner, alone and at peace.

Occasionally someone from the upper levels would come down: curious children or mischievous adolescents. I hated those days. It felt like someone was desecrating my house, violating my space. Thankfully, it was always short-lived—the mist and the maze drove most of them away.

I made one last right and reached one of my favorite spots, close to a broken steam pipe. With a steady supply of vapor spewing out of the cracked tube, this corridor was warmer than most, and in the depths of the mines, warmth had its value.

I sat down against the wall and felt a rumbling against my back. The plumbing in the walls made the only noise on the 22nd floor—creaks and moans and the spewing of vapor. These noises made most people uncomfortable, but not me. I had known these noises for thirty-something years. I found them constant, soothing.

I glanced up at the camera in the ceiling and waved. I liked to think maybe one of the security operators would see me, but the rational side of me knew better. No one was looking at these feeds. There was nothing to see but a thick mist. Besides, most of the cameras down here were dead.

I grabbed one of the two meal rations out of my jacket pocket. Dinner time. Before I ripped open the pouch I could already taste the nutritious mixture, a wonderful change from my daily routine. The perks of a visiting ship, the reason for my journey up top. They always had some extra food on board those ships, food to pay for the temporary stop.

Ardo Station would have been completely abandoned had it not been well-located as a stopping point for long-range missions. It sat more or less halfway between the two closest jump gates in the Maub System. These types of stations were rare in deep space, and a godsend for the poor souls that had to travel through. I was just happy that they kept the place running. I wouldn't know what to do if they ever shut down the station, if I ever had to leave.

I opened the pouch and drank the mixture, enjoying the flavors as they caressed my tongue. What a wonderful combination of senses, a lovely addition to my evening.

A faraway ding interrupted my ecstasy. An elevator had opened. Someone was down here. I felt the frustration building inside me as I put the half-finished ration aside, trying to listen. I hoped it was an empty lift, or a malfunction. I wanted to go to bed soon.

That's when I heard them: footsteps. The sound of boots hitting metal, and yet these were not heavy steps. Even for the distance, they were quiet, soft. Most of all, they were steady. They had a cadence to them, an unwavering tempo. And they were getting closer.

A speaker in the ceiling crackled, then I heard the faint sound of a bell ringing—just one chime. Night had begun. I felt the frustration creeping up once more. How long would this visitor be joining me?

But when the speaker had had its say, only the sounds of Ardo Station reverberated through the corridors. The footsteps had stopped.

I waited a few more moments, then grabbed the meal packet. Maybe I was overreacting. I was tucked away in a far-off corner, and this guest of mine would likely bore or scare well before they reached me. I finished drinking my dinner then placed the empty packet on the ground.

For a few minutes I sat there, listening to the sounds of the 22nd floor, waiting to hear the boots once more. But all I heard were the pipes, the same chorus I had grown used to over the last thirty years.

I curled up against the wall and let myself drift to sleep.

***

The chimes woke me, nine of them this time: the start of the day. Or at least, what we called a day. Ardo was an asteroid quite far from its star, so we didn't bother using the system's time, we just kept our own. Up top they varied the amount of light based on the time, a neat trick to give the human body a circadian rhythm, but deep in my corridors it made no difference. It was just as dark and hazy now as it had been when I fell asleep.

I stretched under the pipe, enjoying the heat for a few more moments before the call of nature had me up on my feet. I power walked down the corridors—left, right, second left, right again. There were seven restrooms down on the 22nd floor, but only two of them still functioned. I pushed the door open and unzipped my bottoms, letting forth the stream of yesterday's filtered liquid and sighing at the wonderful relief.

A faraway noise caught my attention. My body tensed, the relief cut short. Was someone on my floor again?

I strained my ears but heard only silence. Had I imagined it? Something about the footsteps last night had left me on edge, perhaps I was overreacting.

There! More footsteps. Someone was on my floor again!

Something about this did not sit well with me. Every time I had had visitors before, it was in the evening or at night. I couldn't remember ever hearing someone down here in the morning…

I hiked up my bottoms and turned around, ready to confront this new visitor, then froze in place—I could hear them more clearly now: the steps were soft, making little noise on the metal floor, and their cadence was steady… oddly steady.

These were the same footsteps I had heard last night.

Why? Why was I hearing them again?

Then I shook my head and smiled, almost laughing to myself. Who cares why I was hearing them again? The real question was why had I been so worked up? So what if it was the same person? Clearly they had spent the night down here, and now they were probably leaving. I had done the exact same thing for thirty-something years.

Still, I did not want anyone else thinking they could make my home their own. Besides, these footsteps had managed to scare me more than I cared to admit.

I marched out the door to confront this phantom. Fear of the unknown was powerful, fear of the known, not as much.

I stopped just outside the restroom and listened. The footsteps were father away now, and it was clear they were heading toward the elevators. I took off in a sprint, unwilling to let this mystery go unsolved. I knew that sound would bother me for some time if I didn't put a face on it.

I heard a loud ding through the halls and picked up the pace, coming around the second-to-last corner, the last corner… and came to a sudden stop in front of the closed elevator door, without so much as a glimpse inside.

I leaned over, out of breath, frustrated at my failure. Why was I so intent about this? I looked up at the elevators and pressed the call button. I was already here and already upset, so I might as well get my day's ration. I might as well go up top to get it over with.

***

The hangar was accessible from any of the top four floors, and I had chosen the lowest one. Even up top, I preferred to be closer to the bottom. The higher you went, the more people you would see, and I disliked the company of others.

Not that Ardo Station was known for its crowds. The Station's population hovered around 400, a minute amount compared to the thousands that lived here during active mining. Even now, with a long-range ship docked, it would be surprising if we broke 500.

After thirty-something years, you start to learn faces, seeing the same people over and over. I didn't care to meet them, didn't care to know them. Sometimes, the feeling was mutual. I knew I was regarded as the Station rat—the person that lurked in the depths, emerging only for food and other necessities. Most people saw that as undesirable, they tended to shun me. But there were a few people that took an odd pity on me, that tried to help me in their own way.

I hated those people the most.

I walked across the hangar to the staging area, ignoring the few crew members standing about. The strangers always stuck out, and not just because of their clothes: the fact that they were loitering here gave them away. No one else would bother to be in the hangar except to grab their rations.

The offering was laid out as it had been the day before: three crates of food for the Station as payment for three days of lodging. I looked over the pouches, each labeled with their contents. There seemed to be four different meal variations today. I knew each citizen of the Station was entitled to two pouches, and I knew now was the only time the security camera operators took their job seriously. They would be focused on these pouches for the entire duration of the ship's visit. I had to make a choice.

"Come to take some of the food, have ya?"

I winced as a hand hit my shoulder, then ducked down and away, shooting a stern look at the crew member who had been much too friendly. He threw his hands in the air in response, a mix of confusion and frustration in his expression.

"Oh sorry! Didn't know we couldn't be friendly on Ardo Station!"

His eyes told me this interaction was only beginning, and I grabbed the closest two pouches, not bothering to see what I had chosen. Even without this stranger's harassment, my bladder was reminding me that it hadn't finished its job. I needed to get back home.

"What's the matter, don't want to chat?"

I ignored him, turning around and walking across the hangar toward the elevators.

"Where you going?"

His footsteps followed my own, and I picked up the pace. Why didn't anyone understand social cues anymore?

I reached the elevators and pressed the call button, looking up at the displays above, hoping for a short wait. To my surprise and relief, one set of doors opened immediately—there was an elevator already on the floor.

I took a step toward the open lift and felt the hand on my shoulder once more.

"Hey, I'm talking to you."

I tried to move forward but the hand gripped me, forcing me to fight against it. He let go and I tumbled into the elevator, losing my meal packets and bumping into someone already inside.

"Sorry."

I grabbed my meal packets and glanced up at the other passenger. There was something strange about—

"Where are we going?"

I turned to see my pursuer, who stepped inside with a grin.

As the doors closed I took a deep breath, staring at the aluminum and waiting for movement. But nothing happened.

"I said, where are we going?"

I ignored him again and glanced at the panel. Nothing had been chosen. I reached over and pressed 22.

"All the way down, huh?"

I wasn't too happy to reveal my home, but down there I could lose him quickly. Plus, I really needed to go to the bathroom—I had almost wet myself stumbling into the elevator.

We started our descent and I continued to mind my own business. Very soon I would be home, and I would lose him. But if I was so confident I would lose this man, why did I feel so uneasy? Something in the back of my mind…

I looked up at the display and tried to focus. As soon as those doors opened I needed to sprint out immediately—I had a mental map already planned to get me to the bathroom and away from this creep.

Then it struck me. The other passenger. He was facing away from the door. Why was he facing away from the door?

Deceleration grabbed my attention and I looked up to see the display change from 21 to 22. I heard the ding, saw the aluminum begin to come apart, and dashed out at full speed into the darkness.

"Hey!"

Right at the first corridor, then left, then another right. I heard the man running behind me, heard his heavy breathing. I was losing him already.

Down a long way here, then this left. Another right, then two rights in rapid succession, under another flickering bulb. The sound of my pursuer started to fade.

A left, a long run, a right, then I stopped. I tried to breath through my nose to keep the noise down and strained to hear…

The footsteps had stopped, replaced by a laugh. The corridors carried the sound but I knew I had lost him.

"So that's how we—"

An odd gurgle interrupted his sentence, then I heard something heavy hitting the ground.

My heart rate spiked, but I kept quiet. What had just happened?

In the silence that followed I could hear the rumble of the temperature control system and the creaking of the water pipes—noises that had always brought me comfort. Yet this time, something was different. This time, I wanted them silenced.

I could hear my heart beating in my chest, the air moving in and out of my nostrils. What was I waiting for?

That's when I heard them—footsteps, starting up again. It was a familiar sound, one that I had already heard. But not from the man. From this morning.

I froze in place, trying to be quieter than silent, trying to listen to the steps. They were slow, patient… and they were coming my way.

A cold panic came over me and I made another mental map of the 22nd floor. For the first time in my life, I wanted to leave, I wanted to be around others. Something about these footsteps, their soft impact and their steady rhythm…

I closed my eyes to focus. If I had judged correctly, I had about forty seconds before the steps reached me, and the only way back to the elevators was the way I had come, the way they were coming…

No—I could make a loop. I could get them to follow me then double back around a different direction. That's what I would do.

Twenty seconds. No time to waste. I dropped my meal packets and sprinted down the corridor, making two distant lefts before stopping once more.

This was the hardest part. I was halfway through the loop and needed to make sure they were coming around the back side before I came around the front. I didn't want to be caught coming the opposite direction. I stood at the corner of two corridors, my body pressed against the wall with just one eye peeking around the edge.

It took a few seconds for the sound of my own heartbeat and breathing to settle down, then I heard them—they were still following, with no change in tempo, no change in pace. There was something horribly deliberate in the pattern, and I felt a visceral fear, an emotion that had always been foreign to me in the depths of the mines. This was my home… why was this happening?

My heart rate grew as the steps approached. Any moment now and they could come around the corner. Though I was surrounded by steam, I felt a coldness within me.

Maybe ten more seconds… five more seconds…

I tried to see through the vapor under the dim lights, to catch a glimpse of this mysterious character, but my eyes were useless. I could only trust my ears.

I got ready to pull back, the sound of the steps closing in. Any moment now they would appear… why hadn't I seen—

Sheer terror gripped me as I realized that my ears had fooled me. The steps were not coming from in front of me, they were coming from behind. About twenty meters behind.

I screamed, unable to contain my shock, and sprinted the way I came, passing the meal packets and coming around several more turns.

Who was this person? Why was this happening?

I took a left and my foot snagged against something on the ground, sending me forward. My hands came up to catch my fall but the ground was wet and they slipped, sending me face first into the metal floor with a thud, harsh pain spreading from the impact and a dizziness coming over me, dulling my senses.

No—I could not afford to stop. I felt a rush of adrenaline and gained some semblance of self, the darkness in my eyes clearing as I tried to sit up. My hands—they were wet. I looked down and saw blood. Dark red—I was drenched in it. My heart sank. What had happened? Was my head cracked open?

Wait—my hands never touched my head, what was I thinking?

Then I saw what my foot caught: the man, the creep… slumped in a pile… and even in the darkness I could see the cut: a deep slit through his throat spewing blood onto the body, onto the floor, onto me…

It was everywhere. The dizziness gave way to nausea and my urine, having been denied so long, flowed freely into my bottoms. I saw the darkness creeping into my vision once more, threatening to take me away…

Then I heard them. The footsteps. The regular rhythm, approaching. They were close now, almost at the corner where I had just tripped. Calm, unperturbed, they made their way toward me.

I did not think—I reacted. I stood up, pain shooting through my left ankle, the one I had tripped over. It was sprained, I had no doubt, but the adrenaline overrode the pain and I hobbled forward as fast as I could.

My gait was uneven, my steps clumsy. Each time my left foot hit the ground I winced, the pain increasing with every step. I was dragging myself, clattering my boots along the metal corridor. Behind me was a much cleaner sound, an even tempo.

I tried to ignore it, to focus on my destination. I was about two hundred meters from the elevators, five corridors away. I needed to get there, I needed to get up top.

Thirty-something years I had been down here, thirty-something years this had been my home. Mischievous children were one thing, but this? I couldn't come back here now. I could never sleep under the broken pipe again. Thirty-something years…

I didn't know if it was from physical or emotional pain, but as I rounded the next corner, the tears started to flow, salty water coming out of my eyes, distorting the hazy corridor ahead. Why was this happening to me? What had I done?

The left ankle was getting worse now, and I started to slow down with every step. I couldn't keep this up, the pain was too great. Blood dripped from my hands as I hobbled forward, trying to maintain my balance, trying to maintain my sanity.

Then I tried to make a right and found a wall where I expected a corridor.

Clarity washed over me, cold and unforgiving. I was not where I expected. I was lost.

I hobbled forward in a panic, praying for a way out, praying I was close to the elevators. Then I reached a steel door, welded shut. The way into the mines. A dead end.

Emotion overcame reason and I tried turning the valve, tried to open the seal, tried to break the welds. I pressed with both arms, leveraging my body against the wall to get a stronger push, but the valve would not turn.

As I struggled in vain I heard the steady sound, a sound so foreign in my home. I cried, the tears flowing freely as I crumpled to the floor. The pain in my ankle and my head was growing, pulsing with my heartbeat.

And then the rhythm stopped, and I was at peace.

Socks

If you're going to be my apprentice, there's something you need to know: the galaxy is a weird place. You think you know the human race, having spent your upbringing on one or maybe even a few planets, but I promise you, there are always surprises on the horizon. Especially in this line of work.

You're going to spend a fair amount of time in the company of strange people. When one deals in interplanetary trade, particularly of niche items, one tends to jump between far-flung systems on a regular basis. Every planet has its own character; a personality, if you will. It's not just the tint of the star, or the strength of the gravity. On some planets, you shake hands. On others, you smell armpits. An unfamiliar custom to be sure, but who am I to judge an entire world's system of greeting?

At each of my layovers over the years, I've tried to get a feel of the populace: a snapshot of the culture. Some of the things I've seen or heard have been quite bizarre, but one planet stands out above the rest, its history an unforgettable white whale in an ocean of intriguing accounts. Right now, I'd like to share that white whale with you.

I warn you that this is a strange and cautionary tale, a peculiar history of dangerous obsession and the item of clothing that typically encompasses the foot.

Immediately, you may notice a quandary: there are, in fact, two items of clothing that typically encompass the foot. One on the inside and one on the outside. Of course, if we are to be precise—and I dare say we should always try—then the item of clothing that truly encompasses the foot would be the sock. After all, does the shoe not encompass the sock?

We could go down a road of personal preferences that lead to blisters and putrid smells, but I'd much rather assume that you are hygienic enough to leave a layer of cloth between your skin and your soles. If not, that would be a habit to get into before you step in my ship.

But I'm getting ahead of myself. Let's get back to that special planet, a place called Friip. Friip was (and is) a $1.2E_M$ and $0.7E_g$ planet, with a G3V star burning around 5300 K. It was the 47th habitable planet colonized in the Milky Way, with the first human visitors about 350 years ago.

None of this is particularly unique as far as habitable worlds go, but Friip did have a particularly unique set of original colonists. Two separate groups, in fact, that landed at about the same time (each group will claim that they landed first, and both of them would be wrong—the exploratory robots landed first, but no one cares about them, do they?).

One of these groups was your average set of planetary colonists: ambitious if not arrogant, ready to lay claim to whatever riches might reside within or throughout the land. The second group was your typical interplanetary hippy type: knights in shining armor, rushing in to protect the natural environment of this new world, claiming it was wrong to exploit a virgin planet despite the fact that the terraforming process had already violated her beyond recognition.

Astute as you are, you can see that a conflict between these two groups was brewing. And as you no doubt know, conflict is the mother of history—the engine of storytelling. But let me tell you, the way this engine ran… it was a machine unlike any other; the Kovin chamber of stories, if you will.

The first clashes between the exploiters and the hippies went as you might imagine, if what you might imagine is violently. Delegations from Earth tried to intervene, but these were seen as attempts at control over the frontier world, and were met with even more violence. Our home planet looked the other way, opting to let this problem solve itself before it got too involved. Such is the noble wisdom of Earth and its people. Long live the Originals.

This conflict would have played out rather typically, had it not been for one specific quality of the hippy types: they were nudists. I was wrong when I said knights in shining armor. These were knights with no armor whatsoever. Part of their definition of protecting the environment was prancing around naked for all to see.

Now, don't take my tone too personally; if nudity is your thing, you do you—in the privacy of your chamber of course. But the hippy types were much more vocal with their preferences. In fact, they decided that the other group of colonists was desecrating the planet with their clothing. They wanted to eliminate the cottons and the wools, the polyesters and the silks. And then one of these buck-naked beatniks found a way to rid the planet of the capitalist colonists and their corrupt cotton.

It started in small doses: one or two dead exploiters, no sign of struggle, no sign of anything really. Then the problem began to spread. Now tens and tens of colonists were dropping dead and no one had a clue what was going on. There was no discernible pattern in the deaths, save one: each of the deceased wore cotton socks outdoors.

This was not a pattern the exploiters picked up on at the time, but they certainly noted that none of the nudists were croaking. So they did the sensible thing and started kidnapping and torturing their hippy neighbors for information. Now exploiters and hippies alike were dying, the former mysteriously, the latter at the hands of the former, but the answer eluded them all—none of the knights without armor seemed to know what was going on, except that the other colonists were particularly mean. As in, torture and kill mean.

Then, five months into this mess, a capitalist, corrupt coroner discovered a conspicuous pattern among his fallen comrades: they all had what looked like highly mutated hookworms in their feet. Upon further investigation, it was all but confirmed that these little buggers were releasing a powerful neurotoxin into the bloodstream, strong enough to kill a man dead in hours.

Colonies of these potent parasites were found all over the landscape, but there was still one piece of the puzzle that didn't fit: the nudists walked around barefoot on the daily, and none of them were dropping dead. The coroner teamed up with a biologist and both of them asked: what gives?

In the end, it was the exploiters need for decency that cracked the code. They kidnapped a few more hippies (because at that point, why not?) and placed the hookworms all over their body, hoping to see the process in action. But then, something odd happened. The only place the bugs made a move was near the genitals—right about where the kidnappers had forced the nudists to put on some underwear.

After further lethal experiments, an unreal reality was revealed: the worms were unable to burrow through bare skin unless they came into contact with cotton first. Therefore, the people who would constantly moon one another were immediately immune, but if one of those bugs ate even a little bit of cotton, it would then be able to continue into the skin and release its dose of toxin into the victim's bloodstream. Basically, everyone that was wearing socks was dying.

Of course, this was a suspicious and confusing discovery, and after cotton was banned and burned and rubber boots became the norm, the exploiters continued their kidnapping and torture, until finally someone knew someone who knew someone who knew something, and the mystery was unraveled.

You see, it turns out that one of the hippy types was ex-military—a top scientist in a covert bioweapon division. Bioweapons: using nature to kill—the hippy way. Anyway, this character spent decades of his past life working on the perfect final solution: a weaponized worm. The man took your standard, disgusting Earth hookworms and added a potent dose of neurotoxin. When he took up his old hobby again on the Friip, the madman was able to alter the worm's entry vector, making cotton a necessary primer, then voila: peace, love, and neurotoxin.

This mad fool gave the worms a formidable libido, then set them loose in the environment. As planned, the worms attacked anyone wearing socks, killing them within hours of contact. By the time the exploiters tracked down the culprit nearly a year later, the damage was done, and it was beyond repair: the worms had multiplied uncontrollably, covering the planet's surface.

Even the rubber boots weren't enough. During the transition from cotton, the worms evolved, and a new specimen emerged that had no need for the clothing primer. Any nudists that hadn't been tortured were now dropping dead, and two years after the beginning of this bizarre saga, the hippies had all but disappeared. The planet belonged to the cotton-wearing capitalists.

And that, dear boy, is the story of Friip, the planet where cotton is still banned, and where socks are a thing of the past. An interesting tale, no doubt, although I can't say there's much of a grander theme here. In any case, it gives us a reason to visit: smuggling cotton to Friip could pay for quite a few nice meals, don't you think?

Aliens

—FOURTEEN LOG ENTRIES UNTRANSLATABLE—

Personal Log Entry 15
Author: Agent D1
Distance Covered: 8.93%

I think reality is finally starting to sink in. I can see why I was asked to keep this log on a regular basis: we all need distractions, things to keep ourselves busy. Space is a lonely place, even with a ship full of companions. And we are not even a tenth of the way there yet.

I will try to avoid these thoughts as best as I can. After all, I am one of the lucky ones: I have a job to do during the journey. I cannot imagine what it would be like to have a destination-based purpose. If only we had the technology to put people in stasis…

But who am I to complain? We have the technology to cross the stars, to travel light-years within our lifespan. That is a miraculous gift in and of itself. Let us hope we are using it wisely.

—SIX LOG ENTRIES UNTRANSLATABLE—

Personal Log Entry 22
Author: Agent D1
Distance Covered: 12.00%

Despite our best efforts, we have made no progress on the signal. Frustrating, sure, but not surprising. I would never admit it to my companions, but as time goes on I cannot help feeling a seed of doubt growing in the back of my mind. Have we overestimated the significance of these patterns? Are the repetitions no more than a coincidence? Did our original algorithms make one of the most costly mistakes in our species's history?

We have sent one response signal per interval, though with our rate of travel and the distance our signals must travel, we do not expect any answers until we reach approximately 56.55% of the total distance. Once we pass halfway, however, we can no longer turn back. What happens if there is no answer? What happens if we reach a dead shell of a world?

No, I cannot think like that. Our planet's entire scientific community agreed that this was worth an expedition, and they would not have used all of the resources to fund this mission if they were not completely sure. This doubt in my mind is just a product of the emptiness of space, the repetitiveness of my tasks, the boredom of reality…

Hopefully writing this log helps clear my head.

—TWENTY-EIGHT LOG ENTRIES UNTRANSLATABLE—

Personal Log Entry 51
Author: Agent D1
Distance Covered: 33.41%

The original signal is all I can think about, there is nothing else in my mind. Every waking moment is spent contemplating the nature of this electromagnetic radiation, our sign post in the abyss. Before we left, an inordinate amount of time was spent deciding how we might communicate with whatever lay behind this beacon, but even now, a third of the way to our destination, we have no solid leads, only best guesses. The signal was meant to be the key to all of the mysteries: figure out what it means and we figure out how to communicate. But we are no closer to an answer now than we were when we first received it, so very long ago. Will best guesses be enough to interact with alien life?

Ask me again later.

—THIRTEEN LOG ENTRIES UNTRANSLATABLE—

Personal Log Entry 65
Author: Agent D1

Distance Covered: 40.58%

My research has come to a standstill as we deal with the crisis. Agent E3 is now in a quarantined part of the ship, but we cannot proceed with one of our companions losing their minds alone in a compartment. Agent E3's fate is in the hands of the A Agents, but even they seem unsure of how to resolve the situation. How long might it take to fix this? I hate to say it, but I hope it takes a long time. The entire thing is a welcome distraction.

Almost halfway there.

—FOUR LOG ENTRIES UNTRANSLATABLE—

Personal Log Entry 70
Author: Agent D1
Distance Covered: 43.02%

The A Agents have decided to terminate and recycle Agent E3. This is not a shocking development, and yet I find myself somewhat surprised. It is necessary, of course. The psychosis has worsened, to the point where there is almost no recognition of reality. How one could fall so deep into this hole so quickly, even Agent C3 and Agent C4 do not know, but they have recommended that all Agents double their logs and social interactions per interval.

The former should be easy, but there is a tense suspicion among us now. Everyone wonders the same thing: who will be the next to crack?

—THIRTY-EIGHT LOG ENTRIES UNTRANSLATABLE—

Personal Log Entry 109
Author: Agent D1
Distance Covered: 52.57%

At this point I am just writing this so Agent C3 and Agent C4 see that I wrote two logs in one interval. Consider this a log to avoid questions about my mental health.

—NINETEEN LOG ENTRIES UNTRANSLATABLE—

Personal Log Entry 129
Author: Agent D1
Distance Covered: 58.92%

On a whim, I counted my social interactions for this interval. They were triple the previously reported average (from around halfway). Triple! A little good news can go a long way.

I cannot overstate how happy the response signal has made us D Agents. Though none of us would ever say it outright, we were all worried about the same thing: what if the first signal was a fluke? Well, now we can be more confident that it was not. New patterns, new ways to approach translation… this could be the breakthrough we have been waiting for.

With enough luck, we'll keep getting response signals at an increasing rate as we decrease the remaining distance.

—TWELVE LOG ENTRIES UNTRANSLATABLE—

Personal Log Entry 142
Author: Agent D1
Distance Covered: 65.93%

Agent C4 told me I still had to keep a regular log, despite the workload we have. Here it is. Quality stuff.

—FOUR LOG ENTRIES UNTRANSLATABLE—

Personal Log Entry 147
Author: Agent D1
Distance Covered: 67.31%

Two response signals have arrived and still we've made no real progress.

```
—TWENTY-FIVE LOG ENTRIES UNTRANSLATABLE—
```

```
Personal Log Entry 173
Author: Agent D1
Distance Covered: 75.00%
```

Can I hit exactly three quarters?

```
—TWENTY-ONE LOG ENTRIES UNTRANSLATABLE—
```

```
Personal Log Entry 195
Author: Agent D1
Distance Covered: 82.07%
```

The object is going to reach us at approximately 1.24% distance of total distance from our current location. Tension is very high on the ship. If there are entities aboard this object, we still have no way of meaningfully communicating with them, and the A Agents are looking to us for a short-term solution.

So why am I wasting time on this log?

```
—FORTY-SIX LOG ENTRIES UNTRANSLATABLE—
```

```
Personal Log Entry 242
Author: Agent D1
Distance Covered: 93.16%
```

I feel as if we have all of the pieces of a puzzle before us, and yet we do not know how to put it together. The object gave us many answers, but they were not enough to crack the code of the first two signals. But I am not complaining. Despite the continued elusiveness of the signals, we now know that there is bipedal, seemingly-intelligent life on an alien world… this to me seems to be the most important discovery of our lifetime.

No time to celebrate, of course, as we have yet to figure out how to communicate with these lifeforms.

—NINE LOG ENTRIES UNTRANSLATABLE—

Personal Log Entry 252
Author: Agent D1
Distance Covered: 95.61%

The destination world has sent two more response signals in the last interval, bringing the total to sixty-four received signals. Are we yelling out incoherently at each other through the darkness of space, or do these lifeforms understand what we are trying to say?

At minimum, they understand we are trying to communicate. Hopefully that is worth something.

—EIGHTEEN LOG ENTRIES UNTRANSLATABLE—

Personal Log Entry 271
Author: Agent D1
Distance Covered: 98.58%

This mission was a mistake. Another destructive projectile approaches our ship. This is a hostile and aggressive alien species, and they intend to destroy us.

—THREE LOG ENTRIES UNTRANSLATABLE—

Personal Log Entry 275
Author: Agent D1
Distance Covered: 99.12%

Time is running short. The closer we get to the destination, the more the dominant lifeforms attack us. I am so close to understanding the signal, I am so close to finding the meaning behind the mess… perhaps there is an answer to this chaos, perhaps there is a reason for their actions.

But I don't think I have enough time to find it.

—TWO LOG ENTRIES UNTRANSLATABLE—

The series of personal logs above were transmitted out of the alien ship moments before it crash-landed on Earth. Most of the translation work was based off of the alien author's (Agent D1) near-complete work.

Humans

The first signal reached Earth at 14:42 UMT on what is now known as Day of First Contact (or DFC): December 11th, 2081. In order to understand the events that followed, the reader must remember that at the time, SETI initiatives were not nearly as prevalent as they are today. In fact, during the second half of the twenty-first century, most SETI projects were underfunded and undermanned—including the teams responsible for detecting and verifying the first signal. If we summed the number of individuals comprising all of those original groups, their number would not exceed 200 in total. This is in such stark contrast to today that it is almost unimaginable, but it was precisely these low numbers that allowed subsequent events to unfold as they did.

Within minutes of the signal's arrival, intelligence agencies around the globe deduced the significance of what was occurring, and thus began a complex and coordinated international effort to silence each of those nearly-200 individuals.

This process completely reversed and negated existing disclosure standards and remains a highly controversial decision to this day. While the level of obedience to this initiative was surprising (due to the nature of some of the individuals coerced into cooperation), what was more surprising was the cohesiveness of the secrecy given the level of mistrust between countries: most allied nations with knowledge of the signal refused to share their findings or analyses with one another, despite knowing full well that these same allies were already aware of the transmission. Instead, nations worked to spy on one another's work without revealing their own findings (a political climate reminiscent of the Cold War, with many parallels to nuclear programs during and after World War II).

Very few countries broke this secretive mold: the EU was the only major multinational entity that allowed and encouraged open communication between the intelligence agencies of its members, going so far as to inform the respective agencies of any member nations still unaware of the signal and bringing them in for discussion and analysis. This cooperative effort was spearheaded by Germany and France, and their ability to overlook national interest in favor of global (or at least communal) interests should not be understated.

Earth had just under 42 years to analyze that first signal, but the vast majority of progress was made in the first few hours. Before the end of the day, it was understood that the transmission was almost certainly of extraterrestrial origin and possible proof of intelligent, extraterrestrial life. Decades of subsequent research managed to pinpoint an estimated origin, but there was never any true progress on translation of meaning.

As time went on, scientists and government officials alike petitioned for the information to go public, but every campaign for disclosure failed. Over time, there was marginal progress, as some of the most suspicious nations began to share their findings amongst themselves, but these discussions remained highly secretive, reserved only for top government and military operatives.

By 2100, the members of the EU had decided to respond to the transmission, and spent many years crafting a reply. Before they could agree on the content of the response, however, the second signal reached Earth (at 09:22 UMT on September 12th, 2123). Within minutes, it was clear that this signal had come from the same entity, yet the location did not match: the origin point had drifted almost two light-years closer to Earth.

It was after this second message that Rachel Valena, a signal analyst working for the Mexican government, risked her life and publicized both signals with significant amounts of raw data to verify her claim. A week after the arrival of the second signal, the secret had spread across the globe: everyone knew about the aliens and everyone knew they might be coming to Earth. Three weeks after her disclosure, Ms. Valena was found dead in what would later be ruled a suicide (there is naturally some debate about the circumstance of her death, but that discussion is left for other sources).

While there was a great deal of chaos in the immediate aftermath of the announcement, by the beginning of 2124, riots and protests had subsided, and it became clear that the disclosure had more positive effects than negative.

Earth came together in ways it had never done before, and all of those viciously secretive intelligence agencies opened up their doors, sharing their information with one another and with the general public (this was mostly thanks to Ms. Valena, as she had already shared the most sensitive analyses). SETI initiatives at the time surpassed even today's numbers, and there was seemingly endless funding by various governments to be the first to either catch the next transmission (at this point, everyone expected a third), or understand one or both of the first two.

The first mission was simple enough: point more and better equipment toward space, particularly in the direction of the previous signals. The second mission was nowhere near as easy, though it was arguably the most important. There were several false leads over the years, and various groups claimed to know the meaning behind the signals: our impeding doom, the next coming of some god or deity, etc. Each of these interpretations fought against one another, and as different sections of the scientific community tried to convince the general public that their interpretation was the correct one, it became harder and harder to discern the credible theories from the popular ones.

At 12:00 UMT on March 25th, 2130, the UN sent an official reply signal. There was significant controversy surrounding this decision, particularly from a public afraid of announcing our presence, but the consensus was that the entity was already approaching humanity's position —a response signal would not likely change its intentions. This was pure guesswork, of course, but the human race had no true reference point for such a monumental discovery, and the people of the time did what they thought was best.

The third signal arrived at 03:10 UMT on November 1st, 2143, and the UN sent a satellite (Handshake) full of data on Earth and humanity towards the incoming signals, intended to both give the aliens more information about our planet and race and also to give humans an idea of what was coming. It would be several years before Handshake reached its destination.

A fourth signal arrived at 17:55 UMT on April 24th, 2150 and, based on the approaching trajectory of the transmissions, an arrival date was extrapolated: June 8th, 2158. Each signal brought with it a wave of hysteria, but the announcement of the extrapolated arrival date truly hit a nerve: a general feeling of paranoia took hold, and protests and demonstrations against the UN's transmission of replies became increasingly violent. In January of 2151, several scientists working out of an affiliated lab in Nevada were physically assaulted. Just three months later, two members of a small SETI group in Brazil were killed and dismembered, despite no real connection to the UN initiatives.

Meanwhile, scientists and the general public spent significant time and effort trying to translate the signals. Unfortunately, in most cases the signal was interpreted in whatever way fit preconceived notions and, combined with the general uncertainty and chaos of the time, the theory of impeding doom eclipsed all other interpretations.

More and more signals came in at an increasing rate, and less and less time was spent trying to dissect their meaning: most funding had now shifted to defending our planet from potentially hostile aliens. The last straw came with the interception of Handshake: the entire world watched as the satellite's approach was broadcast over the internet (delayed several months from real time due to the distance), but before Handshake could return any meaningful data, it went dark.

This was taken as an ominous sign, and Earth came together once more, but this time in a different fashion: militaries, intelligence agencies, and space agencies from across the globe joined forces to plan the protection of Earth against an entity that was suddenly assumed to be aggressive and malevolent. The theory of malicious intent had become so pervasive and influential that top officials and scientists alike began to support the effort—a veritable snowball effect.

All of this paranoia culminated about a year from the extrapolated arrival date, when the US, acting on behalf of an international agreement, fired several nuclear projectiles toward the unidentified object. This particular decision summarizes the mindset of the time period: the destruction of the entity took priority over the first potential identification of and/or contact with intelligent extraterrestrial life. In hindsight, these actions seem not only absurd, but primitive. Upon closer inspection, however, this should come as no surprise: the survival instinct of the entire human race overruled nuanced thought.

Each of the projectiles went dark moments before contact, and there was no real way to verify that they had attained their target. But when another signal was received approximately a month after the object should have been destroyed (and only two months away from anticipated arrival), several more projectiles were fired.

This second round of fire would provide the first look at the aliens, as the weapons did not lose contact with Earth pre-impact. The video feed showed a large craft of (aptly) otherworldly shape and appearance, although after several impacts it was clear that the projectiles were partially responsible for this odd structure: each nuclear device cut out massive portions of the ship, annihilating the impacted areas completely. The craft's reaction to each missile hinted at technology unknown on our planet: with each direct hit, sections of the ship seemed to collapse upon themselves into nothingness—a bizarre reaction with neither fiery explosions nor projected debris.

What happened next is well-remembered the world over: the alien craft transmitted one last signal as its final section careened toward Earth. The remaining mass was deemed small enough to burn in our atmosphere, yet the composition of the ship defied our understanding and crash-landed near the coast of Alaska.

In the immediate aftermath of the crash, it was discovered that the final signal contained a complicated but roughly translatable segment. While most scientists poured over the recovered remains of the alien ship, the same individuals who had spent their lives analyzing the first few signals finally had the beginnings of an understanding of meaning. After another 12 years of analysis, the logs of Agent D1 were released, and the first true communication between extraterrestrial intelligent life and human kind was available for the world to see.

The translation effort remains contested and many alternate interpretations have emerged, but the original transcript remains the most widely cited and trusted rendition. Many questions remain, three of which comprise the highest priority for present-day SETI research.

First, the origin of the lifeforms: attempts to locate the planet of origin have not yet been successful, and there are some groups who posit that the ship represented the entire population of the species. Nevertheless, most of the planet's antennae are pointed in the same direction, waiting for the next transmission.

Second, the nature of their technology: while the recovered craft has answered many questions, its interaction with the ocean seems to have disrupted some of its original properties. The most pressing question for scientists studying the alien technology is how they managed to travel at the speeds they did with a craft of such small mass.

Finally, and perhaps most importantly, the lifeforms themselves: some groups have proposed that sections or even the entirety of the alien craft itself were an organism; perhaps it was the one communicating with Earth the entire time (these same individuals claim that the main translation, with A Agents, C Agents, etc. is incorrect). None of the transmissions gave any description of their physical appearance (again, depending on the accepted translation).

Another question worth discussing is what might happen if another signal reaches Earth? Will translation be possible? Does the alien race believe in retribution or revenge? Even if they do not, how will the human race react?

There is only one way to find out. If you are listening out there, please come back. We are sorry.

Happiness

2122: Jeffrey & Daniel

The ice made a familiar clink as Jeffrey drew small circles with his glass of whiskey. He brought the shallow pour up to his nose, closing his eyes to enjoy the smell of the beverage. Already he could imagine the rich taste in his mouth, the smooth texture down his throat. What was life without the small pleasures?

"A whiskey man, I see."

He opened his eyes and nodded at Daniel, surprised his friend didn't already know this about him. Had they never shared a drink like this? It was true, their chats were usually earlier in the day, and yet he had imagined them to be so close…

"And you?"

Daniel's hologram sat two meters away, a three-dimensional representation of his body in a chair similar to Jeffery's. Only the occasional flutter of static betrayed the nature of his ethereal form.

"I don't drink."

This was news to Jeffrey. Perhaps he didn't know Daniel so well after all.

"So what is it you wanted to tell me?"

Jeffrey took a sip and let the liquid meander between his teeth and gums, soaking every part of his mouth. After a moment he swallowed, enjoying every minute detail of the experience.

Daniel leaned forward in his chair, flashing a sly smile.

"I've signed up for Peaceful Slumber."

Jeffrey stared at his friend for a long moment, unsure if he had heard correctly. It was as if he didn't know this man at all.

"Really?"

Daniel nodded enthusiastically.

"I put in my deposit this morning. They will begin the set up in two weeks time."

Two weeks? Jeffrey set his glass down on the end table beside his chair. This was a lot of information to process.

"And your partner?"

Daniel leaned back in his chair, a bit of his excitement fading.

"I haven't told her. But she is welcome to join me if she chooses."

Jeffrey felt a growing disgust, but he kept his expression neutral. If someone had asked him to join them in Peaceful Slumber with only two weeks notice…

"Why are you doing this, Daniel?"

As neutral as he kept his expression, Jeffrey's tone gave away some of his distaste.

Daniel frowned.

"I didn't think you would be one to disapprove."

Jeffrey sat up straighter, trying to regain lost ground.

"No no, I don't disapprove, Daniel. I just don't understand. It's all quite sudden, don't you think?"

Daniel shrugged.

"Yes and no. I only have so many years left on this Earth, Jeffrey. Less than I imagine, most likely. I realized there was no time to waste. The ultimate goal in life is happiness—true happiness. And now I can have it for the rest of my days."

Jeffrey couldn't help but frown. This was the same argument he had heard from the salesmen when they had contacted him. Had Daniel really been so easily swayed?

"And your affairs?"

Again, Daniel shrugged.

"I made the decision this morning, Jeffrey. As I said, even my partner doesn't know yet. I will take care of these details over the next two weeks."

Details? Jeffrey raised his eyebrows.

"Shouldn't you take some time to think about this, Daniel? This is a major decision, after all."

He was careful with his words, manipulating his tone so as not to offend the image of the man in front of him.

Daniel shook his head emphatically.

"There is no time to waste, Jeffrey, that's the crux of the matter. Every day I think about it is another day living this mundane life of mine."

Jeffrey did not understand how lying in a bed hooked up to all matter of medical instruments could be less mundane than the glass of whiskey by his chair, but he kept this thought to himself.

Daniel leaned forward once more, his expression growing more serious.

"Did you try it Jeffrey? Did you let them hook you up?"

Jeffrey shook his head.

"No."

The men had been persistent about the trial—too persistent. It had left a bad taste in his mouth, and Jeffrey had been less than polite in asking them to leave.

Daniel gave him an incredulous look.

"No? Jeffrey, you made a mistake my friend. You must invite them back. Five minutes is all it takes. Five minutes and you will be sending your deposit the next morning, I guarantee it."

Jeffrey eyed Daniel warily. That was precisely what he was afraid of.

"I'll consider it."

He wouldn't, but Daniel seemed satisfied with his answer, leaning back into his chair.

"Please do, Jeffrey."

He gestured toward the glass next to his chair.

"Imagine for a moment every sensation that brings you, then multiply that tenfold. Even then you have not reached the euphoria that they can give you."

Jeffrey eyed his whiskey glass with suspicion. Daniel was right of course. As wonderful as each sip was, it was no match for dopamine, oxytocin, or endorphins. Nothing was. Not the butterflies of one's first crush, the rush of sexual climax, or even the love for one's child.

"I'll consider it."

He grabbed the glass and took another sip. Somehow, this second mouthful was not as satisfying as the first.

2189: Melissa

The mechanical eyes stared at her, empty of emotion, empty of understanding.

"I'm sorry, but we are at capacity."

Melissa held back the urge to scream. Yes, she knew they were at capacity. It didn't need to repeat the same information a dozen times.

She took a deep breath before responding.

"When is the next opening?"

The robot hesitated. Melissa watched it, a hint of hope growing inside her.

"I'm sorry, but we are at capacity."

This time, she couldn't hold back. Melissa screamed at the lifeless machine, slamming her open palm against the glass divider. This was not how her day was supposed to go. The next closest sleep facility was ten minutes away.

Ten minutes of cold wind and pouring rain. Ten minutes of crying babies and shouting mothers. Ten minutes of pure, unfiltered reality.

She stepped away from the kiosk and the next person in line shuffled forward. Had they not been listening? Did they not understand?

"I'm sorry, but we are at capacity."

Melissa didn't wait to see how the conversation developed. She walked along the side of the building, staying under the overhang. Every few meters someone would shove into her, each of them refusing to step out into the rain as they crossed paths.

A gust of wind came through the street and she grabbed at her shawl, pulling it tight around her shoulders. What was this terrible weather? What was this terrible day?

"Hey!"

An unfamiliar face shouted at her in anger as their bodies collided, shoving her forcefully into the wall as he passed. Melissa was so used to these types of exchanges she hardly noticed. Her mind was focused on one thing: why didn't the first facility have an open spot?

She reached the end of the path and turned into an alley. The rain tapped the top of her shawl, each drop sinking a bit deeper into the material, threatening to soak into her hair. She knew she could have taken a longer route and stayed under cover, but this alley cut thirty seconds off her trip. Anything to get there faster.

Eight more minutes, she thought. Eight more minutes and she would have thirty minutes of peace. Thirty minutes of pure, unfiltered happiness.

How long had it been since she had last taken a slumber? Five days? Six? However long it was, it was too long. The wage she earned was decent, but it was not sufficient. Thirty minutes of slumber for ten hours of work? She had to find a better job with a better rate. As soon as she used these thirty minutes, of course.

A shrill meow stopped her in her tracks, and Melissa looked down to the source of the noise: a cardboard box, soaked through with rain. She glanced in front and behind her, but there was not a soul in sight.

The box meowed again, and Melissa bent over, grabbing one of the top flaps and slowly pulling it open. Inside was a kitten, its white fur as soaked as the box. It looked up at Melissa with piercing blue eyes, eyes that begged for warmth, for comfort. For a few precious seconds, they shared this moment, the rain still tapping the ground around them.

Gently, Melissa replaced the lid of the box. As she walked away, she heard the kitten meow once more, a piercing noise that dug into her heart. The rain soaked through her shawl, and the drops mixed with her tears as they ran down her face.

Thirty minutes, she thought. Then she'd come back.

2207: Henry & Joanna

Henry took another glance at the digital readout on his living room wall. 18:34. Was this a joke?

"Incoming call from Joanna."

Henry sat up straight. Finally.

"Accept."

There was a quick tone indicating recognition of his command, then the hologram of his sister manifested itself in the space before him.

"Henry."

Her tone was stiffer than usual, not the tone he was used to hearing from his younger sibling.

"Joanna, what took you?"

Joanna sighed, some of the tension leaving her expression.

"I didn't want to have this conversation again."

Henry felt the frustration growing inside him, but he put a lid on it before it could boil over. This was his sister, after all.

"Why, Joanna?"

She paused, raising her eyebrows.

"You know why."

"But Joanna, this isn't just about you."

Some of the frustration had slipped into his tone and he cursed his lack of control.

"Henry, I'm not having this conversation again. I've made my choice."

Henry closed his eyes, taking a deep breath. This was his last chance, he needed to be smart.

"Joanna, please reconsider."

His tone was soft, agreeable, and it seemed to do the trick.

"Henry…"

Henry interjected before she could finish.

"Joanna, listen. Just one. Just have one and then you can take the slumber."

There was a sadness in her eyes as she responded.

"Henry, listen to yourself. Just have one?"

But Henry soldiered on.

"Just one, Joanna. Nine months. Nine months then you can go."

She watched him with a hint of pity, then shook her head.

"I'm sorry, Henry. I'm not waiting any longer."

He could not hold it any longer.

"No, Joanna! You have to! Don't you understand what is happening? Don't you see?"

His sister stiffened at his tone.

"Goodbye, Henry. I love you."

The hologram disappeared, and Henry stared at the empty space that had just held his sister. She was twenty-three… twenty-three! How many people stayed awake past twenty nowadays?

Not enough. Not enough and he knew it. But no one seemed to care.

The Park

I can still remember my first visit, all those years ago. I was two or three —something like that—and my mother told me she had a surprise for my birthday.

"We're going somewhere special," she said.

I remember those words. I remember the excitement I felt when she gave me that smile because I knew… I knew where we were going. Somewhere special? I didn't have to guess.

The trip there was a blur. Like any trip it was full of people and buildings, noise and lights. That hasn't changed. Really not much has changed, has it?

In school I would hear about it, other kids had already visited, some more than once. They always talked about the animals, the little creatures here and there. But when we arrived, I realized none of them had ever really talked about the plants.

They were everywhere! Trees as tall as I could see, bushes all around… I can remember the first time I walked in, running straight onto the green grass, finding a spot between the hundreds of other children and lying down. Putting my face on the soft blades, closing my eyes, and smelling the earth.

Even then, all I could smell were the other children. My parents chided me for putting my face on the ground, but I didn't understand. It was supposed to be natural, wasn't it?

We spent hours in The Park. I wanted to see every corner, every part. I thank my parents for their patience. They let me run the show.

Sure enough, I saw the critters: squirrels, birds, even a mouse. All of the children tried to get a better look, tried to catch them, but they would scurry or fly away before you could get too close. I think my favorite memory was seeing one of the birds fly. It was the first time I had ever seen anything like it: so graceful, so beautiful.

It's hard to look back on that memory now.

I went back at least once a year for almost eight years. Eight years! By the time I was six, I started hearing the rumors. Some of the older kids were talking about it one day, trying to show off their knowledge to us young ones. They told us everything, every detail and every reason. But I didn't listen. After all, my parents told me it was real. Why would they lie?

Of course, now that my son is turning one, I understand completely. There needs to be a little magic in the world, a little hope. That's what The Park represents, after all. The natural world, with plants and animals galore.

A one year old doesn't need to know the plants are fake and the animals are animatronic. They don't need to know that we've sucked this planet dry and we'll never see another squirrel or tree again.

They need a little hope. And sometimes, so do we.

Festival

For the uninitiated, it would seem Percival was in the middle of some sort of partial seizure, or at least victim to a series of facial tics. But any other engineer would understand the subtle movements of his eyebrows, the occasional jump in his lips. Every wiggle of the nose, every blink of an eye… this was a language he was speaking, the language of the interface.

Only he could see the screen before him, a system projected on the surface of his eyes. And as he moved from one section to another, tiny monitors implanted in his brain took note of every synapse traveling to and from the 43 muscles of his face. These signals were translated into his intentions: changes, adjustments, modifications.

"14 periods left."

The interface disappeared, sensing an interruption in the workflow. The muscles of his face relaxed, and Percival closed his eyes.

Why wouldn't they allow a mute function, he wondered. After all these successful performances… could he not get that one kindness?

"Did you hear me?"

His eyes opened and he looked at the woman sitting across from him, his coworker for so many generations…

Time could really make you tired of a person.

"Yes, Genevieve, I heard you."

She smiled that smile of hers, a smile Percival had seen so many times. It was meant to be friendly, but it only served to irritate him.

For better or worse, she never noticed the frustration in his expression. Her eyes were already glazed over, darting to and fro, the subtle movements of her cheeks and forehead letting him know that she was back in a workflow.

Part of him wanted to interrupt her, to startle her with some equally useless information. Of course he knew 14 periods remained—the countdown was the most critical part of this whole endeavor, did she not realize he would be checking it regularly, especially this close to the finish?

He gave her one last look of disapproval then let his eyes lose focus, returning to the interface.

Though they were both working on the same project, their jobs were completely different. Genevieve was nothing more than a master terraformer, one of hundreds and hundreds of her kind. Percival, however, was a star-controller. And he was the only one in the galaxy.

14 periods was not a long time, which made Genevieve's presence all the more annoying. The closer they got to the Festival, the less of a role she played. Of course she could afford useless chatter—she was already preparing for the next one, selecting a few candidate planets and contemplating their pros and cons.

But Percival's role became more and more critical as the periods ticked away. Under one hundred, he preferred not to stray from the interface. Under twenty, certainly not. He could use a little solitude to help his focus —or at least a mute function.

A small alert came up in his display: the neutrino flux was increasing a few percentage points above the desired rate. He switched over to the iron injection line and decreased the feed.

Better to be a little late than a little early, he thought.

"This is going to be my last one, Percy."

Percival left the interface once more, eyeing Genevieve. He hated that nickname.

"What?"

There was something different in her look, a hint of sadness he had never seen before.

"This is it. This is my last Festival."

He forgot all about the horrible nickname. This was her last Festival?

"What do you mean?"

She smiled again, but it was not the smile he knew, the friendly smile that irritated him. The sadness in her look, the sadness in her tone… it was in her smile as well. For a fleeting instant, Percival yearned for that old smile, the one he had dismissed just moments ago.

"I'm done, Percy. This is my last one. After this, a different master will be working with you."

He stared at her, unsure of how to respond. Why hadn't she said anything? Why hadn't anyone said anything?

"But what about right now? Aren't you working on the next observatory?"

She nodded.

"Yes, but I am only laying the foundation for my successor. They will choose where to hold the next Festival—not I."

Percival tried to remember the first time they had worked together, hundreds of Festivals ago, millions and millions of periods ago… Genevieve had been here before him, had helped him ease into the position. She was always so friendly, so kind. And at first, so was he.

A pang of guilt hit his gut, and he looked away from her, unable to hold her gaze.

"Why are you leaving?"

There were hundreds of hundreds of master terraformers, but there was a reason Genevieve was the one sitting across from him: she was the best of the best. She had earned this position after an illustrious and lengthy career, a position Percival knew was considered the highest honor achievable in her profession.

So why was she leaving?

"I am tired of being behind the curtain, Percy. I want to experience the Festival with my own eyes."

He looked back up at her and saw a hunger in her expression, a hunger he could not understand. But he dared not speak unkindly of her desires.

"Besides, it's time I pass the torch to someone else. I can't do this forever."

Percival felt another pang in his gut, but this one was not of guilt.

For so long he had considered Genevieve and all the master terraformers inferior. After all, he was unique—the one star-controller. But what gave him the right to this spot? What storied career did he have behind him? He simply knew a trade that no one else seemed to choose.

Why not, he had wondered. Why wouldn't someone want to be a star-controller? He was the master of the show, the true artist of the Festival. Everyone in the galaxy knew his name!

But he knew the answer to his question, as much as he didn't understand it. It was the same reason Genevieve was leaving. A star-controller had but one purpose, and that was the Festival. Percival would never be able to see his work in person: he had to be behind the interface, managing, changing, adjusting…

A sharp tone brought him out of his thoughts and back to the interface. Another alert. The neutrino flux had dipped sharply. His earlier modification had been too severe, and in the ensuing conversation, he hadn't monitored the reaction.

That familiar frustration came back, and he cursed Genevieve for bringing this up now. They were less than 6 periods away. Her part was over, so of course she was relaxed. She had chosen the planet, molded it to perfection, and now billions upon billions of galactic citizens were on that world, looking up through the engineered atmosphere at a bulging star in the sky.

Each of these individuals was ready to celebrate the end of another million periods, an arbitrary mark of galactic time. It was an excuse to socialize, to revel… Percival didn't quite understand the point, but he would make sure it went off with a bang.

That is, if he could get the timing right. According to the countdown he had just over 4 periods left. He ramped up the iron injection and kept an eye on the flux. If Genevieve said anything now, he would ignore her entirely. These last few periods were critical.

The readings increased steadily, matching his desired path.

"Thank you for everything, Percy."

He kept his eyes on his interface, doing his best to ignore the conflict within him. She should know better, he thought.

"I'll miss you."

2 periods remaining. Neutrino flux was at 10^{47} erg/s. The star was already collapsing in on itself.

"Percy?"

1 period remaining. The supernova was underway. He knew his job was done, knew he could look away, but he wanted to be sure, wanted to know it finished without a hitch.

"What is it, Genevieve?"

His eyes came off the interface moments before the countdown hit zero.

"Look."

He followed her pointed finger to the large display on the wall behind them. A remote video feed showed the star exploding with unimaginable energy, a spectacular show of light to mark the beginning of another million periods.

It was beautiful, he realized. Maybe she was right?

Organism

Twenty eager younglings sat in front of their holodesks, their posture impeccable and their eyes locked on the instructor standing at the podium. The class was nearly silent, the only noise coming from the teacher's desk as he pressed holographically projected buttons that floated before him, each input giving a small tone to indicate its selection.

Today was the first day of courses, and this was the first lesson of the day. Each of the children had spent four years in these academic halls among their older peers, and each one had heard at least one story about the first lesson in Life. Excitement simmered beneath their prim posture, and when the instructor finally closed the interface and saw the faces before him, the clear eagerness brought a smile to his lips.

This was what it was all about, he thought.

"Good morning, students."

"Good morning, sir."

The chorus of young voices widened his smile, and he stepped out from behind the podium.

"This class is called Life, and we are going to spend the better part of a year studying everything we can about this mysterious and fantastic concept, from its origins on Earth through its expansion over the colonized worlds. There's so much information to cover and so little time, so let's jump right in, shall we?"

A few of the students adjusted in their seats, leaning slightly forward in an effort to bring their ears just a little closer. The instructor watched this with a smile, then continued his lecture.

"Today I have a big question for you all, a question that may seem simple or even nonsensical, but I assure you it is neither of those things. It's possible you have heard about this question from your older peers, but I hope they were gracious enough to spare you the details—I would hate for this wonderful lesson to be spoiled ahead of time."

He glanced across the room, honestly hopeful. The older kids had a tendency to ruin all the fun.

"Before we get to the big question, I have two small questions we need to get out of the way. After all, you didn't think you could come to school and not answer any questions, did you?"

A few of the students giggled, and he stepped back behind his podium, activating the display. A large sphere appeared above the class, its surface mostly blue and green, with dashes of white all around.

"Can anyone tell me what this is?"

A small light on each of the children's desks activated, letting them know the instructor had opened the question to all of them. Most hands went up, and the instructor nodded at one of the girls toward the back.

"Yes, ma'am?"

"A planet!"

Her answer was so energetic, a few of the other children turned at the outburst.

"Correct, a planet. But can anyone name this planet?"

Another set of hands. This time, the instructor nodded to a boy in the front.

"Yes, sir?"

"Alpha?"

The instructor smiled.

"No, that's not Alpha. Alpha is more blue. Anyone else? I'll give you a hint: I already mentioned it today."

More hands went up, and the instructor nodded to another girl.

"Ma'am?"

"Earth."

The instructor nodded.

"That's right. Earth. This is what it looked like thousands and thousands of years ago, when humans just began appearing on its surface."

He made a gesture and the sphere expanded, surrounding the children in light. They stared in awe at the display of the ancestral planet, watching its slow rotation.

"Now, before we get to the big question, I have one more little question for you."

He made another gesture and the hologram disappeared. Several kids frowned, dismayed by the sudden departure of the beautiful planet.

"Don't worry, she'll be back. But before we look at Earth again, can anyone tell me what an organism is?"

Fewer hands went up, and the instructor chose a new girl in the third row.

"An organism is an individual entity that exhibits the characteristics of life."

The instructor chuckled.

"Someone already studied the material, didn't they?"

The girl nodded proudly.

"Well, you're right. An organism is an individual entity that exhibits the characteristics of life. Simple enough, right? Well here comes the big question."

This was it, he thought. He knew they knew what was coming, and yet he had their full attention. With another gesture, the Earth reappeared above the class.

"Is this an organism?"

The students stared at the world, eyes wide.

"I want you to really think about the answer, then cast your vote."

A small hologram appeared above every student's desk, asking them to decide if the Earth was or was not an organism. The displays were made in such a way that no student could see what another was choosing. After a few moments, the vote was cast.

The instructor eyed the numbers on his podium and smiled.

"Interesting choices, all of you. For the rest of this class, we will attempt to answer this question, one step at a time. As the class goes on, we will cast new votes, to see if anyone changes their minds. Remember, mistakes are part of learning. Never be too proud to change your answer, but always be sure to understand why you are changing it."

He changed the display to show a balance labelled "Yes" and "No" with tiny weights for each vote. For the moment, the balance was tilted in favor of "No."

"So, if we want to call the Earth an organism or not an organism, we need to be more clear about what an organism is. Young lady," he gestured to the young girl who had read ahead. "Can you remind us what an organism is?"

"An organism is an individual entity that exhibits the characteristics of life."

The instructor smiled.

"Exactly. So, our job is to to figure out the characteristics of life and see if Earth fits the criteria. Can someone name a characteristic of life?"

A few hands went up, and the instructor nodded toward a new boy in the second row.

"Sir?"

"They have cells."

"Correct. Something that is alive is composed of one or more cells. So, was the Earth composed of cells?"

He directed the question at the same boy, who hesitated.

"Sort of…"

The instructor nodded encouragingly.

"Yes, sort of. Some of it is. The biosphere, everything on Earth that was alive, is made of cells. But vast parts of the Earth were not alive. Now here's a follow-up question: are you made of cells?"

This time, the boy did not hesitate.

"Yes."

"Yes, but are you 100% made of cells?"

The boy hesitated a second time, and after a while, it was clear he could not answer.

"It's a complicated question, so don't worry if you're not sure. The answer is no. You have a lot of what are called extracellular matrices: bone minerals, blood plasma… not everything inside of you is made of cells. Only some of you—really most of you—is made of cells."

A few of the kids were nodding, eyes locked on the glowing sphere hovering above their heads.

"Let's return to the question. Based on what you just heard about an organism having cells, does that change your vote?"

The students were given a few seconds to change or keep their vote, then the balance reappeared. A few weights switched places, some going one direction and some the other, but in the end the tilt became more even.

"Interesting. Let's see what happens as we continue. What is another characteristic of life?"

Fewer hands went up.

"Sir?"

"We breath?"

The instructor shook his head.

"Good guess but no, there are lots of living things that don't breath. Remember, you can't think of it as what humans do, but what all life does."

The boy nodded.

"Do you have another guess?"

He paused, clearly deep in thought, then shook his head.

"Here, let me help. There's one called homeostasis. Does anyone know what that is?"

Two hands went up, including the girl that had read ahead. The instructor nodded toward the other girl.

"Yes?"

"It's like, a balance?"

The instructor nodded.

"Very close. Homeostasis is a combination of processes trying to keep things in balance, to keep things stable. Something that is alive will regulate itself, it will keep balance."

He smiled.

"Now here's where things get really interesting: the Earth's atmosphere was not in chemical equilibrium—there was more oxygen than would normally be expected. But that oxygen content was exactly what was needed for life. Another example was the ocean. The salinity was surprisingly low, or, in other words, the ocean was much less salty than you would expect, but, curiously, just salty enough to keep those cells we just talked about alive."

He paused, eyeing the students.

"Let's vote again."

The process repeated, but this time, weights moved only from the "No" to the "Yes," which was now the slight favorite.

"Look at that—the balance has shifted. But hold on, there are many more characteristics of life. This question isn't answered yet. Can anyone think of another characteristic of life to help solve this mystery?"

A few hands went up.

"Yes, sir?"

"They… reproduce?"

A few of the kids giggled, but the instructor continued unfazed.

"Yes. Something that is alive can reproduce, multiply. I am glad you brought this one up, because this one is, in my opinion, the most interesting. I mean, there's no way the Earth can reproduce, right? It's a ball of rock, after all."

Some of the kids nodded.

"Let's vote again, knowing that reproduction is a characteristic of an organism."

This time, there was a dramatic shift to the "No" side, with only four weights remaining stubbornly in the "Yes."

"Case almost closed, it seems. But now I'm going to try to defend these four rebels, and argue that the Earth can reproduce. In fact, I'm going to argue that it already did."

The students leaned in closer once more, clearly intent on hearing how it was possible a planet could multiply.

"If we say that humans are part of the Earth—that all life was part of the Earth—then you could say that when we spread out onto other planets, that was Earth reproducing. Right?"

One of the kids shook his head.

"You disagree, why?"

"Because… we're humans, not the Earth. There isn't another Earth, we just moved to other planets."

"Good answer. I mean, if there are birds living in a tree and they move to a new tree, did the tree reproduce?"

Now most of the class shook their heads.

"Okay, but here's another question. Are the birds part of the tree?"

More head shaking.

"Right, the tree did not make the birds, but the Earth made humans. And I just said that life was part of the Earth, that humans are part of the Earth. So even though we didn't reproduce its rock, we did reproduce parts of it."

He could see some of the kids slipping away, a cloud of confusion coming over their expressions.

"It's a weird thing to think about, right? I can see some of you disagree, and that's good. But stick with me, because I'm about to make it even more crazy."

The confusion faded, replaced by that earlier enthusiasm, that earlier curiosity. Some of them knew were this was going, some of them knew the climax of this tale.

"There are so many things in this universe we do not understand, and life is one of them. Is the Earth itself alive? A tough question to answer, but here's something interesting to consider. Did you know plants communicate? That's right, the trees, the grass, the flowers… they talk to each other with airborne chemicals and networks of fungi in the soil. It's fascinating really, and it makes you wonder… all of this information, all of this chatter, it could be the planet expressing itself. I mean, so could animals communicating, or even humans."

He was losing them again, so he paused.

"Sorry, everyone. I'm losing you, aren't I? Let's take the poll again. Who thinks the Earth is an organism, and who doesn't?"

A few weights shifted back to the "Yes" side, and when all was said and done, the "Yes" side was only three less than the "No."

The instructor smiled.

"So I know all of you are eager to hear the real answer, to know whether or not you got it right. Well, I have some news that's both good and bad: none of you are necessarily right or wrong. Humans like to define and classify things, it's in our nature, but life cannot be so easily organized. There are other characteristics of life that we didn't discuss, and using these other characteristics, there are ways to argue Earth is an organism, and there are ways to argue that it isn't. In the end, whether or not Earth is an organism depends on how you define life or organisms. You might say that makes this more of a Language lesson than a Life lesson, but let me assure you that knowing how to think outside of the box and understand things from all kinds of perspectives is the most important Life lesson of all."

Theseus

When I was seven years old, I fell out of a tree and broke my arm. I remember the moment well, though I can't recall any pain. I'm sure there was some, but the pain I remember came later, during the weeks it took to heal. You know: rest, medication, the usual components of a so-called natural recovery.

Natural. What a funny word. What does it even mean for something to be natural? The definition is an oxymoron, a paradox. Existing in or caused by nature, not made or caused by humankind. Who came up with this explanation? Humankind is a part of nature, everything is. We're all made from the same stuff: carbon, nitrogen, oxygen… those byproducts of supernovae. Every plant, every animal, but also every piece of litter, every non-biodegradable plastic, every kilogram of radioactive waste… all of that came from the stars, all of that exists or is caused by nature. By definition, all of it is natural.

But I digress. The point is that the healing process was slow, annoying. It was weeks before I could use my arm normally. And all because I was young.

You see, in the old days, it used to be that being young meant you could heal faster. In some cases, being young meant you could heal at all. But now? This whole healing naturally thing is a vestige of the past, and you can bet your ass I'm not forcing my kids to go through that crap. If my son breaks his arm, he's gonna have it replaced. Bing bang boom. Two days max, and he's back to normal.

I mean, why not? That's the world we live in now. Those are the options we have. Why would I try to prolong his suffering? What kind of father would that make me? The only problem is going to be hiding it from his grandma.

It was my mother's idea that I heal naturally, and what she said was law. My father knew he wasn't going to be all that involved after a few decades, so he didn't bother arguing. What was the point? I've always wondered what he thought of natural healing, what with his propensity to replace body parts, but I lost my chance to ask him many years ago. I guess I could try to find him now, but who knows if I'd even recognize the man? And would either of us really care?

Modern medicine is a double-edged sword, that's for sure. I'm not going to go so far as to say that my mother was right, that I should have healed slowly, but I will say the way we live our lives now… I certainly do my best to avoid injuries, to avoid these replacements. But some things are just out of your control.

I was fifty-six when the choice was taken out of my hands. Fifty-six! The first step to my future, though at the time it seemed like my last. Malignant mesothelioma. Can you believe my luck? Less than 10% natural survival rate, that doctor told me. Those words, I remember. That conversation was much more painful than breaking my arm.

And again with that word. Natural. Are modern procedures, the products of years of miraculous developments in tissue engineering and cloning, unnatural? After all, when I got the diagnosis, I knew what happened next. They took those cells they had, those stem cells from when I was a baby, and they grew me a new pair of lungs. A brand new set of breathing organs, just like the doctor ordered! And then wham, bam, thank you ma'am, and the transplant had me on my feet, mesothelioma free just a few weeks after the diagnosis. And most of that time was spent letting the lungs grow. Transplant recovery time? Two days. Crazy.

But there was a reason I avoided injury, a reason I was none too happy with my diagnosis, even knowing full well I would be cured. Those replacements? They keep on happening. There's no way to avoid it, short of dying naturally. Naturally. But who does that anymore?

A few years later, it turned out the cancer wasn't actually gone. A little bit of it had stuck around and snuck into my kidney. That bastard. The doctors told me this one had better odds, that I could do it the natural way. But they also told me I shouldn't. They hinted that getting a replacement was the cleanest way to do it, and the only way to be sure. I thought to myself, why waste months of my life dealing with another natural recovery? I had endured the broken arm, let's switch out the damn thing.

So I said okay, let's do it, but can we please make sure nothing else is compromised this time? I'd rather not do this every few years (in hindsight, a hopeless expectation). They said okay, did a few tests, a few scans, and said I should be good. I don't think they were very thorough, and frankly, I doubt they really cared. Why waste your time checking when you know you can replace something if you're wrong?

And they *were* wrong. A few years after I replaced one kidney, I had to replace the other. I was getting used to this process, and truth be told, I felt great afterward. These were organs made from my old cells and barely aged—I was turning back the clock, living with pieces of me from my twenties.

But I also knew this process never stopped. There was always something falling apart, needing repairs. Over the next twenty years, I got a new pancreas, new small intestine, even a new heart. New eyes, new teeth, a new scalp for my hair: you name it, I got it.

And that was just the beginning! Eventually I opted for a full musculoskeletal reconstruction, including all major muscles, bones, ligaments, and tendons. That took a few years, but it added at least fifty to my lifespan. Then came the circulatory system, and a complete blood supply replacement. The skin, all of it was remade—the best cure for wrinkles, let me tell you. Finally they hit the peripheral nervous system, probably the most complicated of all.

Well, all except one. The final frontier. The brain.

The brain had been an enigma for so many years, and for good reason. Most of the procedures I had undergone were the byproduct of hundreds of years of research in tissue engineering. The business exploded decades ago, with wealthy individuals pouring unfathomable amounts of capital into the industry to recapture their youth. Here I was, nearly a hundred years later, reaping the benefits of what they had wrought.

But the brain could not be replaced like a heart or a lung. If you grew a new brain, even from my cells, it would not contain my consciousness, my personality, my memories. It didn't work that way. And good luck to any scientist trying to figure out how to "copy/paste" that kind of thing from one to the other. It might be data, but we aren't robots.

Enter cloning. When researchers realized tissue engineering wasn't going to get them where they wanted to go, they tried to clone brains and, hopefully, clone consciousness in the process. Instead of "copy/paste" it was just "copy."

The experiments started with animals, as they always do, and slowly but surely made their way up the chain. Man oh man was that a slow process. Ethical complaints increased with each step, and once we started reaching the higher forms of animals, there were real concerns that the experiments would have to stop.

But progress is unstoppable, particularly with an ocean of money behind it, propelling it at breakneck speed. My father was a key figure in this ordeal, one of these elite individuals intent on immortality. You see, he was one of those billionaires, and he had undergone all the procedures I eventually received, but decades earlier, when they were still new. The man was nearly 200 when I was born, an event that, according to my mother, was the product of a momentary existential crisis during the lapse in progress. He wasn't sure if they would solve the brain problem in time, if he would be able to keep living.

But they did. Using the technology of the cloners and the engineers, scientists were able to create young brains imbued with old souls. The final frontier had been crossed, but at what cost?

My father is not alive anymore, and yet he is. He went in to have his brain copied, and the doctors and robots made a new one for him, a new one with all of his memories, all of his personality. They put the new one in and voila, he has another hundred years under his belt.

But is that really him? The old brain was discarded, as was the old heart, the old lungs, the old veins, the old eyes... No part of that man is original, and yet every part of that man is derived from his cells. But he isn't alone. We are all the ships of Theseus, sailing infinitely in our quest for immortality. It's just human nature.

I think I'll go ahead and get the new brain.

Type IV

"There's always a bigger fish."

He grinned at me, a grin that was all too natural, all too real. I felt sick.

"What do you mean?"

"I mean you are not at the top."

I could feel the back of my mind disagreeing with this situation, a nagging sensation that beckoned me away. But another force, much stronger than my own will, kept me on the matter at hand: the person—no, the thing—in front of me.

"I… what?"

He frowned, shaking his head.

"I already told you, don't try to resist. It will only bring discomfort."

I hated him in that moment, but that moment was fleeting.

"Does it have to be like this?"

He shrugged.

"No, but it is easier like this."

It's not easy for me, I thought. Shouldn't he know that? If he was controlling all this, shouldn't he be able to tell?

"Anyways, like I was saying, there's always a bigger fish. We are the bigger fish."

Bigger fish? Did this thing even know what a fish was? Why did he look so human…

He frowned.

"You're not paying attention."

"Sorry."

I wasn't really sorry, but right now, I didn't control my reality.

"Aren't you curious? Don't you want to know more?"

I barely heard the question. I was staring at his face, that perfectly human face. My brain kept telling me to relax, that this was normal, but I fought against it. I knew this wasn't a human, I knew this wasn't a conversation. I didn't know what this was, and yet at the same time I did.

He sighed, giving me a frustrated look.

"Do you need me to explain this to you again?"

He could read my thoughts. At least, it seemed like it.

"No. No you don't."

A second explanation wouldn't be any better than the first. Nothing could accurately describe this experience. Talking with an alien that had hijacked my mind to communicate with me using a visual representation of my own species and my native language to help mediate the connection? And he wondered why I was having trouble wrapping my mind around it.

"Why me?"

He sighed.

"You're wasting time. I have much more important information to tell you."

I tried to tell myself it was a dream, or perhaps some drug-induced vision. But I knew that was a lie. I knew this was real. Of that I was sure, more sure than I had ever been of anything, ever. How and why I was so sure, I had no idea, but I guessed that this thing in front of me—this thing that spoke to me with a human face and human eyes and human lips—had something to do with it.

"Your species is quite an odd phenomenon."

This caught my attention, and I gave him a confused look.

"What?"

He smiled, happy to have brought me out of my musings.

"Ah, that self-assuredness is under attack, that brings you to the now. But that's why I am trying to tell you there's always a bigger fish."

Enough with the fish!

"Okay, you're more advanced. I get it. Why are you here?"

He shook his head.

"I am not there. I am simply there."

He pointed to his head.

"In you. But me—my actual, physical body—is far, far away. Millions of lightyears."

I stared at him. How was that possible?

"You're wondering how, aren't you?"

He *could* read my thoughts.

"I know you are. It's a good question. And why I am here, also a good question. But there are better questions, bigger questions. I have the answers to those questions. Aren't you curious? Don't you want to know more?"

He was right, of course. I was curious. Yet I had a hard time letting myself agree with him.

He sighed, shaking his head.

"Let go of your pride. It has no place here."

There was no way he couldn't read my thoughts. But if he knew what I was thinking, why bother with this conversation?

"What do you want?"

He smiled.

"I am here to help your species by answering some important questions. Not why you are the one I am talking to—this is not important, this is irrelevant. I am here to tell you about things that are almost beyond your comprehension. About the past and the future, about the universe and its secrets. I can help you start to pull back the veil, to see a little more of what lies beyond. But you can't be so proud, you can't be so stubborn. You aren't the biggest fish. You're less than a fish, you're a worm in the water. You are insignificant and fragile, but that's okay."

I found myself growing angry at this being. If the human race was so insignificant, why was he communicating with me? Then I wondered: was he communicating with anyone else? I could ask, of course, but why bother? More than likely that was one of the "irrelevant" questions.

I took a deep breath and let the air out slowly.

"Ok, tell me."

Why fight it? I had no choice. Let him say what he has to say and be done with it. This was uncomfortable, but maybe if he said what he wanted to say, he would let me go.

"I can't tell you yet. You need to relax. You need to accept that you are insignificant, that you are secondary. Your species is much too proud, much too arrogant. A big fish in a small pond, but this is the universe. You're in the ocean now."

"Enough with the fish!"

My restrained anger came out all at once and I felt the immediate shame that one feels after reacting too strongly. I wanted to look away but I simply couldn't—there was nowhere else to look.

He gave me an amused look.

"So stubborn. So upset. Your kind will have trouble adjusting to this knowledge. You may self-destruct within a few centuries, that would be a shame. But the universe will move on without you. We will move on without you."

I glared at him, the shame erased and my patience gone. Why did he insist on this point? Why couldn't he just say what he had to say?

"You are angry, I can see. Fine, I will relent. I will answer something for you. Do you know why I am talking with you now?"

I continued to glare at him, expecting some kind of trick, some kind of ichthyological analogy.

"I thought that was irrelevant."

He smiled a smug smile.

"Ah, it is irrelevant why I am talking to you, to you the person, the individual. But the timing of the conversation, why it is happening now rather than earlier or later, is relevant."

I could barely hear his words over that self-satisfied expression. If I could hit him, I just might.

"Your anger grows, I see it in your eyes. That's fine. Just listen to what I am saying. You may not have noticed, but your species has reached type one. That is why I am here, that is why we are talking."

"Type one?"

I gave him a confused look, and he returned the gesture.

"You're not familiar with the Kardashev scale?"

Now I stared at him, my eyes widening.

"No…"

My response was not to his question—I knew exactly what the Kardashev scale was—it was one of disbelief. We had reached Type I?

He nodded with a smile.

"Oh, but you have. Just moments before I entered your mind."

I couldn't believe it. We had reached Type I? According to this thing in front of me, the human race was at full planetary energy potential. We now had the ability to harness all of the Sun's energy that reached the planet's surface. It was a milestone we knew we were close to achieving, but I had no idea we were this close.

In that moment he simultaneously answered one of the irrelevant questions: I began to understand why he was talking to me, me the person.

"This is a humble milestone, but a milestone all the same. If your current trajectory holds, you will reach Type II quickly, perhaps even in your own lifetime."

Now I gaped at him, shocked by his words. There was no way. A Type II civilization was able to harness all of the energy of their parent star. He was claiming that before I died, the human race might be able to use all of the energy output by the Sun.

There was no way that was possible!

"I can see the anger has turned to disbelief, I'm glad we are making progress."

He smiled that same smug smile, but I barely noticed. My mind raced, trying to process what I was hearing. For some reason, I had an urge to trust what he was saying. I began to think maybe he wasn't just spouting off nonsense about fish.

"This is a time of an explosion in technology, something that has accelerated exponentially for some time. You know it very well, don't you?

But what you might not know is just how much is yet to come. This will not stop. This will grow, and it will grow fast. And that is also why I am here. I am here to impart some wisdom, a few words of advice from the bigger fish before things get out of control."

I no longer hated him, and I didn't even mind the aquatic references. I was fully focused on what he had to say.

"Out of control?"

He nodded.

"You are not the first and you will not be the last to reach Type I. I am also confident that you will reach Type II. But rare is the species that successfully jumps all the way to Type III, and there is a reason for that: self-destruction."

Type III: a civilization capable of harnessing the energy of their entire galaxy. That was truly the realm of science fiction.

"Self-destruction? What do you mean?"

"I mean that this technological explosion can have both positive and negative effects. And let me be clear: it is up to you, the human race, to decide what is negative and what is positive. To some degree, self-destruction may be a desired outcome."

I gave him an incredulous look.

"How so?"

He smiled.

"A surprise to you, I'm sure, but as your species matures, you will realize that growth and consumption can never end. Many decide that they have had enough, and allow themselves to extinguish quietly into the night. There is nothing wrong with this decision, it is your own to make."

I stared at him.

"And you?"

"What about me?"

"You did not extinguish? What level is your species?"

His smile widened.

"Now you are asking the right questions. Type IV."

"Type IV?"

What was he on about? There was no Type IV.

"You're not familiar with it?"

I shook my head.

"What, you can harness the energy of the universe?"

He shrugged.

"In a sense. Although in some ways, we are the universe."

Now he had really lost me.

"I told you I would tell you things at the edge of your comprehension. And truthfully, I doubt I can be very clear with my explanations, but I will humor your curiosity."

Again, he had my full attention. I still wondered if I was the only one he was talking to, but at this point it didn't matter. I wanted to hear everything he had to say.

"We have managed to encode our existence into exotic, subatomic particles. The same stuff you know as dark matter."

I was gaping again, and he laughed.

"Hard to believe, I know. Give it a few billion years and you might understand."

"You're… dark matter?"

He nodded.

"That's us, yes. And if you want a little more information to fry your brain, we're also responsible for dark energy."

"Dark energy?"

Again, he nodded.

"Remember what I told you about consumption and growth? This is the fundamental constraint on all life that expands. Our best solution so far has been to expand the universe itself, though that does come with its own issues. We can only hope to figure out the details within the billions of years we have before we run out of room."

He paused, looking at me, then laughed.

"You are much more pleasant now, I must say. There may be hope for your species yet."

"Is anyone else Type IV?"

He leaned back in his chair, peering at me. After a lengthy pause, he shook his head.

"No. And you know why?"

"Why?"

"Our existence prevents it."

I stared at him once more, unsure of what he meant.

"You don't understand? It's not too complex. We reached Type IV first. Again, there is only so much room for growth. If a Type III is to jump to a Type IV, it will need multiple galaxies to spread, but we are actively making that more and more impossible as we expand the universe. So it's our fault."

"That's hypocritical, isn't it?"

He laughed again.

"Is it? You speak of the arrogance, the pride?"

I nodded.

"I disagree. There is no arrogance, no pride. We are simply the biggest fish, so we reap the benefits. Remember, I did not say expansion and growth were inherently negative. I said you had to make that decision on your own. We have decided that we desire to do so, and so we continue. A simple analogy would be your own race's expansion, which led to the extinction of nearly all of the other species on your planet. This extinction will continue, if our example is anything to base this analogy off of."

"Then why are you here?"

He grinned.

"The same question, and yet different. You are wondering why we are pushing you forward if we plan to stop you in the end?"

I nodded again, and he shrugged.

"Call it boredom, call it charity, call it whatever you want. At some point, we may merge, who knows? More importantly, a lot can happen in several billion years, and you'll have to survive at least that long for us to be a threat. Until then, we can help you, or at least frustrate you with infrequent visits."

He smiled, but I pressed on.

"You mean to return?"

"Perhaps, perhaps not. For now, I've given you a glimpse behind the curtain. When you reach Type II, we will come back and pull the sheet back even further. Make no mistake, we want you to succeed. It's always more interesting that way. But as you no doubt can already tell, I wouldn't place too much trust in our desire for you to succeed. We have our own intentions, some of which we may never share."

Was this really happening, I thought to myself. Was I having this conversation with dark matter? Maybe this was a drug trip after all, that would make a lot more sense…

"Trust yourself. The others will."

"What others?"

But he was gone, the situation was gone. I was back in my office, staring at the screen in front of me. A readout of our energy potential: a thorough analysis of all of the Earth's resources, usage, etc. And in that analysis, the big number: 10^{16} Watts.

Type I. Only three steps to go.

Conservation

"I can't believe we are even having this conversation!"

Janco threw his hands up in the air, looking around the chamber for support. He couldn't be the only one that cared about this, could he?

"Senator, please. A certain level of decorum is expected in the Senate."

The Arbiter gave him a weary look, but Janco ignored it. This was more important than their damned etiquette.

"This is our home, our origin! And the lot of you are content to watch it disappear forever? You should be ashamed of yourselves!"

"Senator!"

This time, the Arbiter's voice could not be ignored, and Janco turned to face him.

"If you do not temper your behavior, you will be silenced. If you want your message to be heard, I suggest you communicate it more convivially."

Janco held the man's gaze for a few moments, then nodded.

"Yes, Arbiter."

The Arbiter nodded in reply, then turned to the rest of the chamber.

"Does anyone have a response?"

Several lights illuminated, and the Arbiter pointed to the first.

"Senator Voue of the Munnen System, you have the floor."

The woman's podium turned green and she gave a nod in reply.

"Thank you, Arbiter. As others have said, the cost of this proposal is astronomical, simply beyond our resources. We cannot allocate such a large portion of our budget to conservation efforts. While I understand Senator Janco's fervor, and I share in the pain of this forthcoming loss, I cannot condone such a massive diversion of resources. Put simply, we must think of the present at this moment, not the past."

Janco made to speak, but a sharp look from the Arbiter kept his mouth shut.

"Thank you, Senator Voue. Does anyone else have a response?"

Janco pressed the button on his podium and its outline lit up in bright white, alerting the Arbiter to his desire to speak. Of course, Janco knew he wasn't going to be chosen: he had opened the debate with his own call for action, and now it was time to hear the chamber's responses or questions. He could only answer direct questions—any other reaction he wished to give would have to wait until everyone else had had their say. But he did not press the button expecting to speak. The white outline of his podium was more a symbolic gesture than anything, one that ran the risk of angering the Arbiter further.

Thankfully, the man at the front ignored him and pointed to another of his colleagues.

"Senator Rijj of the Way-2 System, you have the floor."

The man's podium turned green and he gave a nod in reply.

"Thank you, Arbiter. I wanted to bring forward a question for Senator Janco."

The Arbiter glanced at Janco.

"Senator, I want to remind you that you are required to answer the question presented to you. No more, no less."

Janco felt the anger growing within him. This was a losing battle, and the Arbiter's chiding tone was not helping his cause.

"Yes, Arbiter. I understand."

The Arbiter nodded.

"Go ahead, Senator Rijj."

"Thank you, Arbiter."

Janco watched Rijj, fully aware of what was about to come out of the man's mouth. He knew what Rijj would ask him, he knew what he was trying to get at. Why were they wasting time with all this nonsense? They needed to act now, before it was too late!

"Senator Janco, could you tell me what the most recent and most accurate models predict for the success of this proposal, and the longevity of this success?"

Janco swore he could see a smug smile flash across his colleague's face, but he waited patiently for the man to pass the floor. With a small gesture, Rijj passed the green light from his podium to Janco's.

"Thank you, Senator Rijj."

He gave a side glance to the Arbiter. How was that for decorum?

"In answer to your question, the most recent and most accurate models predict success at a rate of 96%."

Janco pressed the button to return the floor to Rijj, but the Arbiter shook his head.

"You have not answered the question, Senator Janco."

His podium lit up green again, and Janco sighed, trying to keep his composure. This was such a gigantic waste of time.

"According to these models, the 96% rate is viable for up to ten thousand years."

He passed the floor back to Rijj again, who nodded.

"A follow-up question, Senator Janco: what is the success rate for one hundred thousand years and for one million years?"

The floor came back to Janco but he said nothing, staring at his colleague. Why were they doing this? How could they do this? Did they not see the importance of what he was trying to do? Did they not understand at all?

"Senator Janco, you have been called to answer a follow-up question from Senator Rijj. Do you have an answer?"

Janco glared at the Arbiter then nodded. Without looking at Rijj, he replied.

"The success rate for one hundred thousand years is 47%. The success rate for one million years is 12%."

A murmur went off in the chamber, and Janco could feel his number of allies thinning. To hell with them. Why did the success rate for such a long time matter? Voue's claims of budget constraints were overstated. The galaxy's wealth was increasing at an exponential rate. Did they not think that within the next five thousand years, they couldn't come up with a better solution for the long term? Of course he preferred to have a permanent fix from the start, but this was the best they were going to get… were these clowns fine with throwing away their heritage?

"Thank you, Senator Janco."

Rijj left the floor, and the Arbiter eyed the chamber once more.

"Thank you, Senator Rijj. Does anyone else have a response?"

One podium lit up.

"Senator Dryx of the Bana System, you have the floor."

Her podium turned green.

"Thank you, Arbiter. I too have a question for Senator Janco. Two questions, to be precise."

The Arbiter nodded.

"Go ahead, Senator Dryx."

"Thank you, Arbiter."

She turned to face Janco, who gave her his full attention. He knew Dryx was one of the good ones, or at least one of the neutral ones. She had made large contributions to his previous conversation projects, and he had expected her to help him now.

But the frown she gave before she asked her question made his stomach drop. Had he made the wrong assumption?

"Senator Janco, what is the current state on the surface? What remains to be conserved?"

He stared at the woman in shock. So many responses came to mind, none of them addressing the question at hand. His eyes jumped to the Arbiter, who eyed him sternly. He could not speak his mind right now, he had to watch his mouth.

"Most of the surface is dead, there is no more life. A few megastructures remain, particularly below ground, but their structural integrity is minimal."

Dryx nodded.

"Senator Janco, do you not think your proposal surpasses our action boundaries for interference in planetary lifecycles?"

Janco sighed. Her first question made sense. This one only served to waste time, like all the others.

"I disagree. I would argue this is the one and only exception to these regulations. This is not a project I propose for every planet, for the hundreds of colonized worlds. This is a special case, and we all know that."

"Senator, just the answer please. No more, no less."

He gave the Arbiter a spiteful glare.

"Yes, Arbiter."

The Arbiter turned his attention to Senator Dryx.

"Thank you, Senator Janco."

She left the floor, the frown never leaving her face.

"Thank you, Senator Dryx. Does anyone else have a response?"

Janco was running out of options. He knew he couldn't hold back much longer, not if he had to listen to the Arbiter repeat the same phrases, pushing the discussion forward at a snail's pace while the Sun rocketed toward its terminal threshold at a dangerously unpredictable rate. If they wanted to make this work, they needed to get to work now. Not in a year, not in a month, now.

"Senator Janco, you have the floor."

Janco snapped out of his thoughts, somewhat surprised that there were no further objections, no further holes to poke in his proposal.

"Thank you, Arbiter."

He barely looked at the man at the front, his eyes scanning the chamber from one colleague to the next, searching for a receptive face, a friendly smile… but no one would hold his gaze.

He knew this would be his last chance to make his case, and he knew his fury, bubbling underneath the surface, would only make things worse. He had to be smart here, he couldn't let his emotions take control.

Janco took a deep breath before continuing.

"Senators, I understand there is opposition to this project, and I understand that much of it is rational."

He looked to Senator Voue.

"While it is true that this project would require an unprecedented augmentation of our conservation budget, I disagree with the theory that the cost is prohibitive. Our society is in a period of unparalleled growth, and our wealth shows no signs of slowing down. On the contrary, available resources are on the rise, and nearly every system's economy is booming. Put simply, we are at the most economically healthy point in our galaxy's history. So much so, that we can afford to allocate the required sum of money to this project."

He paused, letting his words sink in.

"Furthermore, for the long-term projections, I repeat my earlier argument. We are at a time of prosperity and growth. Within the next ten thousand years, I am more than confident that we will discover a more permanent conservation solution, but this is by far the best option we have now."

His words were impassioned, and he knew they rang true. And yet even as the faces turned to listen, even as his colleagues lent an ear to his cause, he saw no true persuasion, no victory on the battlefield.

"Most importantly of all, we cannot afford to wait. If we hesitate, if we continue to stall with these political machinations that have stretched out for so many decades, we will run out of time. We must act now, or she will burn up forever. We don't have a second chance on this."

He looked across the sea of faces, finishing with the Arbiter. The man at the front was frowning, but it was no longer a frown of contempt. There was pity in his eyes, a pity that struck like a knife.

"Thank you, Senator Janco. We will now vote on your proposal."

His podium turned off, and the Arbiter started a quick speech on the voting procedure.

But Janco wasn't listening. His mind was on the lonely planet, hundreds of light-years away from the Senate, the once-blue dot that was now threatened by its yellow star.

The Earth would die, and no one was willing to save it.

www.ingramcontent.com/pod-product-compliance
Lightning Source LLC
LaVergne TN
LVHW010840120826
845149LV00017B/3410

9780986314322